D1249917

The Seeds of Doubt

One day, a farmer planted two seeds. The first was a magical seed that could grow into anything it wanted. But the second was just a regular tomato seed.

"I don't want to be a tomato plant," said the tomato seed. "They're ugly and taste terrible. I want to be a blueberry bush. I want to grow blueberries."

"Blueberries do sound good," said the magical seed. "But I'm not sure. Apples are good, too. So are bananas... There are so many options, I just can't decide."

"Rub it in, why don't you!" cried the tomato seed. "You can be anything you want! I'm stuck like this."

Two weeks later, the tomato seed had grown into a small sprout. But the magical seed was still a seed.

"Maybe I'll end up liking tomatoes," said the tomato sprout. "...No. I won't. I don't want to grow tomatoes. I want to grow blueberries."

"A blueberry bush does sound nice," said the magical seed. "But what about an orange tree? Or maybe a grape vine..."

"Enough already!" yelled the tomato sprout. "I don't want to hear it. I wish I was you! You don't know how lucky you are, getting to be whatever you want! Just shut up!"

The two didn't speak after that.

As the end of summer drew nearer, the farmer came and dug up the tomato sprout to put it in the greenhouse.

However, the magical seed was strong, and could brave the winter outside.

A month later, the tomato sprout had become a fully grown plant.

It looked down at itself in anger and disgust.

"I don't want to grow tomatoes," said the tomato plant. "I hate the farmer for planting me. I hate being a tomato plant. I want to grow blueberries!"

Things would continue this way for some time.

Week after week, the tomato plant wished to grow blueberries.

Week after week, its tomatoes only multiplied.

Month after month, the tomato plant wished to grow blueberries.

Month after month, its tomatoes only grew larger.

Suddenly it was summer again, and the farmer came to return the tomato plant to the garden outside.

The tomato plant looked over at its neighbor—at the plot of land where the magical seed had been. It had been so long, the tomato plant had forgotten all about it.

"I bet it's off in some extravagent garden now," said the tomato plant, bitterly. "Probably growing an exotic fruit, or... Or blueberries! Hahaha!" It laughed bitterly.

The weeks came and went, and slowly the tomato plant produced fewer and fewer tomatoes. And the few it did grow were much smaller than before.

In a way, it was happy. But mostly, the tomato plant just felt tired.

When fall approached once more, the farmer came and took the other plants inside.

The tomato plant was so lost in thought, it didn't notice it had been left alone.

A week later, the tomato plant could no longer grow anything at all.

Over and over, it looked to its neighbor's plot, and wondered what could have been.

"I don't want to grow tomatoes," said the tomato plant. "I want..." It trailed off.

It didn't have any energy left to complain.

The tomato plant thought again of the magical seed:

Right now... it was surrounded by other magnificent plants...

It had blossomed into some tall, wonderous flower... and had been whisked away to the fanciest garden in the world...

That is what the tomato plant imagined.

But the magical seed had never left.

And it could've grown into anything, too.

[Scan this QR code to buy this book on Amazon.]